CW00741843

10 9 8 7 6 5 4 3 2 **1**
First Printing

9112000253082

Table of Contents:

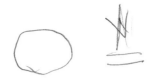

The Story of Yard Dog
Chapter One

1. Meet the Fords.

Once upon a time, far, far away on the sunny Island of Jamaica, lived a happy little dog called 'Buddy', how he became known as 'Yard Dog' the leader of the Yip-Yap Crew, in a far off land called England, is a tale I hope will keep you reading at the edge of your seat.

Are we all ready? Then I'll begin.

The setting for this story is England but starts all the way in Jamaica, New Kingston, 'Palm Lane'. The kind of lane where the good Doctors Glen and Rita Ford and their 3 children, two girls named Pam and Jan and a son name Jon Jon. They lived a good life, in a nice house with a swimming pool and grounds. Jon Jon being the youngest of the Ford siblings by ten years is the family favourite.

The good doc had given up on ever having a son to carry on his name. (Grown up's, think about things like that, you will understand one day). When Jon Jon came along, to say the good doc was happy would be an understatement; he was over the moon, ecstatic.

Jon Jon was denied nothing, you would have thought the child would have been spoiled but he wasn't; he was a very kind and considerate boy, loved by everyone who knew him.

He had a fondness for animals and was always bringing home strays, to be fed. But after his father found out Jon Jon was feeding his best 'Rib Eye' steak to the local mutts, he put his foot down.

I remember hearing a story from one of his sister's, as a five year old, he would take his mother jewellery to school to give to his teacher as presents. They would always return the items to his mother when she came to pick him up at the end of the day; needless to say, his mother had a word with him about his generosity.

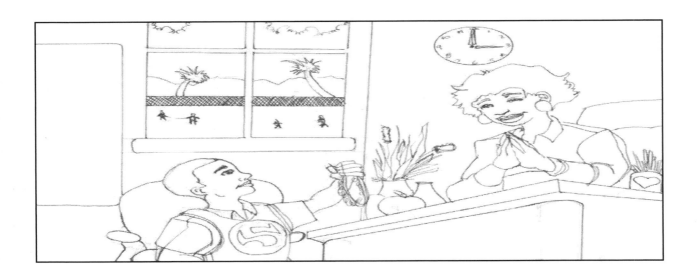

On Jon Jon eight birthday, he asked his father for a puppy, so his father took him to the local dog pound. It was the choice of the puppy that had everyone alarmed, out of all the puppies in the dog pound, Jon Jon picked out a funny looking mongrel.

Not only was it the only mongrel in a dog pound full of fine pedigree's, it was a puppy brought back to the dog pound for being too much trouble; his previous owner felt he was far too intelligent and mischievous but Jon Jon had made his mind up, and that was that.

He named the puppy dog Buddy! So now Jon Jon had someone who he could pet and look after and Buddy for the first time in his short life, had someone who loved and looked out for him.

It wasn't long before they were a well-known double act wherever you saw Jon Jon you knew Buddy wasn't far behind.

2. Buddy grows.

Every afternoon at three o'clock, Buddy would make his way to the school gate to wait for his Master so that he could walk him home. They would do Jon Jon's home work together, which Jon Jon's parents found amusing, until they realized their son had taught the dog to count and read, along with all the other tricks this funny looking dog had picked up for himself. Buddy was proving to be a very unique little dog. Whenever the good Doctor had visitors, Jon Jon and his pet would be asked to put on a show, they never failed to amaze.

All the neighborhood kids loved hanging out with Jon Jon and Buddy; they would play music and sing and dance. Here are some of the lyrics:

'Who's the best dog in town? Yard Dog! Yard Dog!'
'Who's the dog that won't let you down? Yard Dog! Yard Dog!'

Most of the family had a soft spot for Buddy, except for Jon Jon's mother's older sister 'Aunty'; you know the type, tough on the outside and soft on the inside with a heart of gold. Being his mummy's oldest sister, her voice had to be heard and Aunty wasn't backward in coming forward with her opinion, don't get me wrong, she liked the dog; she just felt he was far too pampered, she never liked that Buddy would sleep in the house but there were times when she thought no one was looking she would fall under Buddy's charm and find herself petting him, she would even bring him a big juicy bone sometimes when she came to visit.

Whenever the Fords had to go out of town or on holiday, Buddy would stay with Aunty, she would never admit it but she loved having the dog over to stay. It was on one of his stay over's at Aunties Buddy found a new world; a world that would open his eyes to how other dogs, who were not so lucky to have a Master like Jon Jon, lived.

At Auntie's however, Buddy would sleep in a kennel out in the backyard at night, where the howling of the street dogs from the near by alley-way would keep him awake. Buddy didn't know what to make of this at first. Lately as fate would have it, Buddy had been thinking that maybe Aunty had a point, maybe there wasn't enough 'dog' in him; after all, he did spend most of his time with the Fords.

All he knew the sounds he heard calling him, was like nothing he had heard before. Maybe it was time, to follow his own star.

The warm Jamaican nights had sky's that were full of them; all he had to do was pick one.

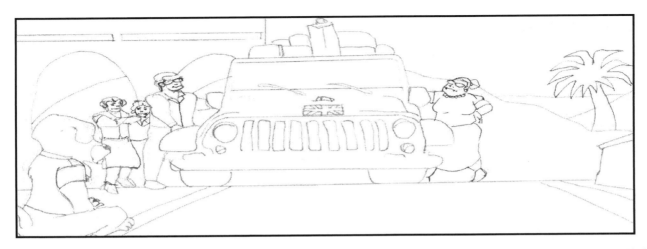

Meanwhile, the Fords were getting ready to go on their annual holiday. This year instead of going to Miami, U.S.A; they decided to go to London, England, U. K, something about looking for a house to buy over there, Buddy wasn't paying too much attention to the conversation, all he knew it meant, he would be spending some more time at Aunties. It didn't bother him as it did in the past for he had made up his mind, he was going to find out about the dog howling he heard at night, where it came from and how he could find the dogs that were making such a racket so he could find out why, they might need help.

They say, 'curiosity killed the cat'*, let's hope that doesn't go for little dogs or our story will be a lot shorter than we expected.

3. Buddy finds 'Dog Lane'.

Jon Jon and his family went on their holiday and Buddy went to stay with Auntie. Two nights passed and he hadn't heard a sound.
"Have they moved them on?" Buddy wondered.
The third night however, the howling started and true to his word, Buddy followed the noise to a few blocks where he came to a dimly lit alley-way. He had found them and his life would never be the same.
When I tell you the name of this place you're going to say
'I'm pulling your leg, it was named 'Dog Lane'; they say humans went down there at their own risk. Dog Lane was a place strictly for dogs, real dogs . . . dogs from the street.
At first Buddy was a bit frightened he didn't know any of these dogs; he wasn't brought up the way they were. Then he remembered what Jon Jon always told him. 'To get by in this world, you have to know how to get on with all different kinds of people, from all different walks of life*'. What a wise little boy! Buddy thought maybe it was time he put that theory to the test. He stood at the entrance, looking down into Dog Lane when one of the dogs spotted him.

"Who's that up there looking on us?"

When the inquisitive mutt saw it was another dog, he seemed to relax a bit; Buddy wasn't sure if it was a ruse just to give Buddy a false feeling of security, until he heard another more welcoming voice.

"Come in my boy" said a rather large dog.

"What happened are you shy?" asked another.

Buddy took a few more steps into 'Dog Lane,' and as they do, all the other dogs with their tails waging ran to greet him.

"Where do you come from?" another asked him.

"He looks clean"', said the first dog, with a smile.

"What has he got?" Let me take a look", said a short stout dog with a mean face. Just as he was about to step to Buddy a big voice boomed. "Back off boy!" Leave the boy alone… You always want rob everybody?"

"No boss, no, not at all boss, I I just wanted to see what he's got".

The short stout dog replied ever so meekly,

"You just wanted to see what he's got," The big dog dressed in black with the big voice repeated in a mocking tone. "Just go sit down and don't move until I tell you. Do you hear me?"

"Yes boss I'm going to sit down right now boss, see I'm sitting down boss. Is here alright to sit down boss"

The big dog kissed his teeth loud and long, not even Aunty kiss her teeth so loud and so long, this must be the 'Don' of 'Dog Lane', thought Buddy as he looked around the lane and at the other dogs.

Buddy found out later that night, the big dog dressed in black was name 'Don Sonny' and he was indeed the Don of 'Dog Lane' and most of the other lanes on that side of town.

Needless to say, Don Sonny liked Buddy; he thought he had guts to come to 'Dog Lane' all by himself. He also took time to introduce Buddy to all the other dogs. What was more important he introduced Buddy as his 'little brethren' that meant no one, and I mean no one, could do Buddy any harm or diss him in any way. They knew they would have to talk to Don Sonny and Don Sonny didn't play!

They had funny names. There was a pair of brother's called 'Chip up' and 'Chap up', another pair where named after two old time legendry Jamaican comedians called, 'Bim' and 'Bam; 'they were the joker's of the pack. Another was called 'One Bite' because he bit his master once and the master put him out.

Then there was the nasty one of the pack who Buddy had met already, his name was Bully Dog. Bully Dog was an old Police dog from back in the day and being such, he felt he had the right to 'bad up' the rest of the dogs as the feeling took him.

From the moment Don Sonny had put Bully dog in his place, Bully dog didn't like Buddy, he blamed Buddy for his loss of face; and whenever Don Sonny wasn't about, he would always try to run him off, but Buddy wasn't having it, he stood his ground.

It may seem that he was spoiled and pampered but Buddy could hold his own in a fight, however he never liked fighting. Jon Jon had always told him, 'It's better to use your head, than your fist, you will last longer, stand up to bullies as most bullies are cowards*.

Buddy, would never tell Don Sonny what Bully Dog was doing as he didn't want to look like a cry baby. The other dogs from 'Dog Lane' respected that and Buddy was welcomed down 'Dog Lane' any time.

As a matter of fact, if a long time passed and they didn't see Buddy, Don Sonny would send one of the dogs to go and look for him just to make sure he was alright. In Don Sonny, Buddy had truly found a friend.

He kept out of Bully Dog's way if he could; it didn't seem smart to make more fuss than was necessary after all he was only a visitor.

Like what he used to hear Jon Jon's father say,

'Duppy know who to frighten'*.

So any time he was staying at Auntie's, Buddy would go off into the night and make his way to Dog Lane, to learn the ways of the 'street dog'. If he knew how much the lessons would serve him, well, how could he know, how could any of us know.

4. The Big Move.

The Fords came back from their holiday with an announcement.

'They were going to live in England! It seems the 'good Doc' had been made an offer in England that was too good to refuse. Also the girls loved it there, they loved the English boys and the English boys loved them. They couldn't wait, to get back to London.

It was only Jon Jon and his Mother who were not too keen on making a permanent move to England. His Mother however, went along with the plan after her husband assured her; it wasn't going to be forever.

Jon Jon was a different matter; he had Buddy to think about… who was going to take care of his dog? Aunty was alright for a short time but he couldn't see Buddy living with her permanently, he might run away and what would become of him then? Jon Jon wondered.

Jon Jon asked his father, if he could stay in Jamaica. He could go and live with Aunty, he suggested to his bewildered family. His Mother told him that her big sister was too old to take care of a young boy and a dog also she would worry about him too much. She was also a bit hurt Jon Jon would want to stay with Aunty and leave her for the sake of a dog. His Father wouldn't even hear of it, he told his son.

"You're coming with us, any more talk of this and we'll get rid of the dog altogether … you hear me boy?" "I hear you sir", replied Jon Jon.

So, not even six months after returning from their holiday, the Fords were packing up again to make the big move to London, England.

Come the day, Aunty decided that Buddy could come to the airport to see them off with her.

Jon Jon, assured Buddy that he wouldn't forget him and asked him to be a good dog for Aunty, as Jon Jon, didn't want Aunty to take him back to the dog pound. Buddy promised that he would be a good dog.

Suddenly! Aunty started to cry at the thought of losing her baby sister, I don't mean some little sniffles; I mean some big wailing so much so, that when Jon Jon's Mother saw her sister in tears, she joined in too. When the girls saw their mother crying and holding onto her big sister, they started to cry also. "Imagine someone trying to take you from me" Pam asked, Jan through her tears. When Jon Jon saw his mother, Auntie and his two sister's crying, as with most families, he started to cry too. When Buddy saw Jon Jon crying, he started one piece of howling in the airport that all the dogs nearby who heard him, started howling too. All the people in the airport began to get nervous, to put a stop to all the drama, they let the Ford family on the plane early and run Aunty and Buddy out of the airport. When Aunty asked why?

"You are causing too much excitement," explained the old airport porter as he escorted Aunty and Buddy to the exit door.

5. Getting involved.

Now that Buddy was living at Auntie's, his visits to Dog Lane grew more frequent and you know what they say . . . 'familiarity breeds contempt*'. Contempt is what Bully dog had for Buddy big time, he never said why. Anyway! It came to pass, that Don Sonny, the 'Don' of Dog Lane' had to leave town. It was only meant to be for a short time but when he didn't turn up for any of the 'dog meetings' they went to look for him but Don-Sonny, couldn't be found anywhere. Bully Dog, took this as a sign to take over and run things his way. Without Don Sonny to look out for Buddy, Bully Dog was soon planning revenge, dogs have long memories you know.

Let me tell you Bully Dog wasn't like Don Sonny who let a dog have a living. Oh no! He was meaner than a 'junk yard' dog and that was mean. All the dogs from Dog Lane and the other lanes near about, had to pay up and pay on time. You had to wonder, how many bones can one dog eat? All the dogs who didn't 'play ball' with Bully Dog after a time would disappear, no one ever knew what happened to them no one knew Bully dog was getting his old Police Master to set the 'Dog Trappers' on them. The Dog Trappers were the most feared thing in a stray dog's life. For one dog to call the Dog Trappers on another dog however was one of the lowest thing, a dog, could do to another.

Buddy didn't have to worry about Dog Trappers because everyone knew he was loved and wanted, that only made Bully Dog hate him more.

As no one had seen or heard from Don Sonny for some time, Buddy decided there was only one thing to do and that was to go out and look for him. After all, how many times had Don Sonny done the same for him? Buddy, noticed that none of the other dogs seemed that bothered when he asked them why? They told him, 'it is just their way, being dogs 'n' all' they also told him, 'he thinks like a human too much.'

"You're too kind. That not going to help you down Dog Lane, that's not going to help you at all." Bim told him; needless to say Bam was in total agreement, "That's true my boy, that's true".

Real talk or no real talk, what he didn't know, every word spoken between Buddy and Bim and Bam was reported back to Bully Dog, by his faithful side kick 'One Bite' Bully Dog as we all know, was waiting for the right excuse to do something to Buddy.

Bully dog had tricked the other dogs from 'Dog Lane' into believing, he was worried and wanted Don Sonny to come back however, Bully dog knew what had happen to Don Sonny, as it was he who had set him up for the dog trapper's in the first place.

As a dog, Bully Dog could get away with a lot but he couldn't get away with setting the dog trappers on Don Sonny if the other dogs found out, there would be consequence and repercussions.

As Bim did remind Bam. "We are dogs, my boy, not rats, there are some things even we wouldn't do" Bam was in total agreement.

"True my friend, true".

"Well why don't you two help me look for Don Sonny?" Buddy asked.

"We're too busy looking for food." replied Bim.

"Can't you see that were hungry?" asked Bam.

"We don't have any time to go and look for anybody," said Bam."

"I'll make a deal with you", said Buddy.

"What kind of deal can you make?" Asked Bim with more than a
bit of curiosity.

"You two help me find Don Sonny, and I will take you somewhere you
can eat till you content." Buddy replied.

"You're messing with us." asked Bim, getting excited.

"You're telling lies," said Bam laughing.

"Do you think I'm joking?" asked Buddy getting serious; he didn't think
this was time for jokes. "I said I will take you somewhere you can eat,
'This dog keeps his word", he told Bim and Bam.

"Alright alright. Don't get upset, we will help you."

Bim and Bam was as good as their word. They had found out that Don Sonny had been captured by the dog trapper's and he was in a bad way, they had beaten him because he had tried to escape.

They also found out that Don Sonny was betrayed, by one of the dogs from Dog Lane. Only one of the dogs from the lane, would know where to find him and at what time.

"Who would do such a thing?"

Bully Dog asked everyone at the last dog meeting.

"We have to find this dog, for this dog is not a dog, this dog, is lower that a wharf rat." He concluded as if 'butter wouldn't melt...'

All the dogs agreed whoever this dog is; He was truly lower than

'a big wet wharf rat'.

Buddy agreed with everyone and acted as if he believed Bully Dog's two faced words. He was wondering, were Bim and Bam really taken in by Bully dog? How far could he trust them? Remembering what they said "After all, they are dogs!"

"Can I ask you something?" Buddy said to Bim and Bam.

"Do you really believe the Bully dog?"

"Believe what", replied Bim.

"Didn't your mother ever tell you to take time when your taking your head out of a lion's mouth?" asked Bam*.

"Do you think that we want to end up like Don Sonny? Anyway, we helped you find out about Don Sonny, where is the food?" asked Bim, licking his lips.

"You did" replied Buddy with a smile "Come with me".

True to his word, he took them to a place where there was a lot of food, I don't have to tell you where he took them, do I?

That's right! He took them to Auntie's and they had a belly full. If Auntie never came and caught them and run them out of her house, they might still be there eating her out of house and home.

"Wait! The dog gone mad!" Aunty, shouted when she saw Buddy, Bim and Bam in her kitchen, she ran for her big licking stick, she gave Bim a lick on his side, as he was running through the back door.

He was limping for a week but he said it was 'worth it' as he hadn't eaten like that for a long time. Buddy knew he was in trouble when he got home. If the truth be told, he wasn't sorry that Bim got a lick, that way, he knew they wouldn't bother him to take them back there.

You know what happens when you 'feed a hungry Dog' don't you? Yes that's right! "He keeps on coming back".

6. Story a come to Bump.

After the meeting broke up, Bully dog sat alone thinking, he didn't
believe he had fooled the one Buddy for one moment.

"That dog is too smart, for his own good and mine. I'm really going to
have to do that dog something."

Meanwhile, Buddy tried to get back into Aunties' house without her
seeing him… no such luck.

"I'm waiting for you, how you mean to bring back your riff raff into my
house. Have you gone mad? Look at the mess you've made in my
kitchen, what am going to do with you?"

Aunty was well vexed, but to Buddy surprise she didn't make as much
fuss as Buddy was expecting.

Buddy didn't feel too good about what he had done but he gave his
word and Jon Jon always told him 'your word must be your bond'*.

The next day was like most days in Buddy's happy life it was a Sunny day, without a cloud in the sky. If Jon Jon was here, it would be a perfect day, it doesn't look like Jon Jon is coming back home for now, Buddy thought to himself as he was walking down the road, he stopped to say "Hi" to some kids who knew Jon Jon.

"When was he coming back?" one of them asked.

"Soon," replied Buddy, "soon".

"You take care of yourself," they told him.

"Thank you" he said as he set off merrily on his way.

All off a sudden, he felt a shocking pain up side his head, by the time he knew what was going on a barrage of licks was raining down on him. He was taking a beating, he got in a few licks but 'trust me' he was taking a beating. Bully Dog, had caught him off guard.

"I bet you thought I wasn't going to 'get you'?" Bully Dog asked as he kept on beating him, "Where is your big bad 'Don Sonny' now?"

It was the kids who knew Buddy was Jon Jon's dog, who came and ran him off. Bully dog would never try and bite any of them, as he knew that would mean him being put down, no questions asked.

It was a good thing too, who knows where this beating might of ended. When Buddy got to Auntie's house, he tried to fix himself up, he didn't want Aunty to see him in such a state… no such luck.

"Wait! What happen to you? Who did this to you? Asked Aunty all in one excitable breath. Buddy didn't know what to tell Aunty he just stood in front of her with his head hanging down, when Aunty saw how Buddy looked so defeated, she shook her head and said in a much more sympathetic tone of voice, 'come my little 'Yard Dog' come let me fix you up'. Buddy never knew where Aunty got that name from or why she really called him it, as he only slept in the back yard whenever he was staying at her house. He knew however, she only ever used the name when she was trying to be affectionate and that 'will do, right now' Buddy thought, he was in pain after his run in with Bully Dog.

God bless Aunty, he said to himself, as he followed her into the house. Aunty put some ointment and bandages over Buddy's cuts and bites and gave him his supper. She also let him stay in the house for a few nights until his wounds were beginning to heal.

Everyone was talking about Buddy's misfortune. He was made to look like he couldn't take care of himself and Buddy didn't like that one little bit.

There were two old women, friends of Auntie's, who came to the house the next day to visit. What they had to say caught Buddy's ears… well most of it.

"Look at him, look how he's messed up." said the first lady.

"Good gosh how can you be so wicked?

'Can't you see that he is sick?" Replied the second lady.

The two old ladies's started to laugh at Buddy's misfortune.

"He's not sick, didn't you hear he went down to Dog Lane being nosey and a bad dog beat him up."

"What is this you telling me?"

"Yes Miss's, you know, I wouldn't lie."

"Oh my gosh! What is this I'm hearing? What a shame, such a nice little dog, why didn't they take him to England?'

"Don't be such a fool? Do you think you can just take a dog to England?"

"Why can't you, miss know it all?"

"You're not going to understand but trust me you can't",

"I heard England is a land of dog lover's"

"Maybe, but they have enough dogs over there to love, they don't want anymore but its true what you're saying, they do love dogs."

Now, that was the part of the conversation that got Buddy's attention,

the part about England being a land of dog lovers.

Maybe Jon Jon didn't know about this England being a land of dog

lover's; if he did, he would have taken him for sure, he thought,

all Buddy could think about for the rest of the night was England,

England, that's where I should be in England with Jon Jon.

7. … Always dig two.

Buddy had reached a turning point in his short life, he knew if he took the wrong bend in the road now there would be no turning back.

It was time to start thinking with his head not with his heart or pride.

It was he who had taken it upon himself to hang out at 'Dog Lane' and mix up with the dogs he met there. Ever since Jon Jon and family had gone to England, Buddy thought he had found a new family and it felt good to belong to a gang at times. But this turned out to be the wrong gang and now it was time to do the right thing and move on.

He remembered another saying of Jon Jon's father (Doctor Ford loves his saying's and philosophy, maybe we should collect them all; I'm sure you kids will find they'll come in handy, as we all need words of wisdom to guide us sometimes). Anyway, as I was saying, oh yes!

The saying, it went like this 'Whenever you're going to dig a pit, against your fellow man (or brother), don't dig one, always dig two.'*

As Buddy lay by his kennel thinking things over Auntie's voice broke his thought.

"Are you going out today?" she asked.

No! Not today" he replied, trying to sound nonchalant so Aunty wouldn't know anything was wrong, but there was no fooling Aunty.

She took a seat on one of the veranda chairs, picked up Buddy and put him on her lap as she stroked the top of his head.

Buddy was surprised as she had shown him so much affection lately; being a pet he had to admit he liked it but it only made him miss Jon Jon more. As she was petting him, he noticed she began mumbling something to herself.

"They've gone to England! They've gone to England!"

When it dawned on Buddy what she was saying He asked.

"Aunty, why didn't you ever go to England… didn't you want to know what England is like?"

"Who told you that I don't know England" she replied

"Aunty, tell me bout England, is really a land of dog lover's?"

"Yes they love dogs, when I was there it felt sometimes that they love dog more than they love us."

"What makes you say that?"

"It was a long time ago, the world was a different place back then I did suffer a great loss" she said.

The memory of her time in England must have been painful, as she petted Buddy, he looked up at her and there was tears rolling down her face. He tried to comfort her the only way he knew how, he began licking her face she gently pushed his head away so he would stop licking her but kept hugging him, she asked.

"You miss Jon Jon , my little Yard Dog?"

"Yes Aunty I miss him alot."

"Never mind, you will soon see him again don't worry."

"Aunty I want to go to England."

It was the first time he had said it out allowed and it felt good.

"What are you talking about, you're a dog, you can't go to England, who told you this foolishness?"

She stood up gave Buddy one more kiss on his forehead and put him back on the ground where she found him.

Aunty went back into the house and Buddy was once again left with his thoughts. All of a sudden he heard a voice he knew but it couldn't be. What would they be doing here? It was.

"Hey! What's happening Bro?" a familiar voice called out to him.

It was Bim and Bam.

"What are you two doing here?" Buddy asked them.

"Wait! Aren't you glad to see us?" Bam asked him.

"We come, to warn you," said Bim.

"Warn me about what?" asked Buddy.

"We come to warn you about Bully Dog, said Bim, in a most excitable tone of voice.

"So you better watch you're back, you know how sly he is... look how he catch you off guard; if the children didn't run him, who knows what would have happened" said Bim.

"What do you mean? Bully Dog would have mashed him up," said Bam not holding anything back or trying to spare anyone's feelings.

"And if He ever finds out we came to warn you, He's going to mash us up too", said Bim, who seemed to be getting frightened at the thought of Bully Dog.

"It's not like you two to help anybody... what's in this for you?" Buddy asked, with a grin.

"You can stay and grin you teeth, this is no joke" warned Bam, who also seemed to be getting paranoid at the thought of Bully Dog finding out they had warned Buddy.

"We're going now, come on", said Bim looking around as if they might have picked up a tail.

"You're so shook." said Bam, in a mocking voice.

"Just let Bully Dog find out we came here and you will see who is shook just come on'',said Bim as he pulled Bam down the road with him.

"Take care, you hear?" they both said in unison as they hurried down the road. Bully Dog was looking for him, now Buddy had a lot to think about as he lay in the sun. Just as Bim and Bam took off down the road Aunty came out to see who was in her back-yard with Buddy.

"Wait! You bring back you're riff raff to my yard?"

Buddy was still thinking and he didn't even notice Aunty or what she was saying, he looked up at her and said.

'Aunty I'm going to England'

"You're going where?"

"I'm going to England"

"Didn't you hear that you can't go to England... who's going to take you?"

"I'll go by myself"

"Alright you tell me why you have to go a England so bad, you just tell me, e".

Buddy never said anything to Aunty.

"Does it have something to do with you, going down to 'Dog Lane'?"

It was no use he could never fool Aunty, she had a way of seeing through him, from day one.

"Yes! One of the bad dogs is looking for me, him say he's going to done me, also, I want to see Jon Jon too,"

"So you're running away from a bad dog from 'Dog Lane?"

"I'm not running from him, I should be frightened but I'm not, that's what I find worrying. I don't want to do this mad dog anything and mash up my life. So I think I should go somewhere for a while".

"It's a pity; you never did think before you start go to 'Dog Lane', next time think before you act before you drive me mad".

"You're right Aunty I will remember that but for now I have to get away from here and I'm going to England, I don't know how, I don't know when, it will be very soon but I'm going to England and I'm going to find Jon Jon".

How was Buddy going to pull this one off what was waiting for him in the future?

In Chapter 2 you will find out.

The end of chapter one.

The Story of Yard Dog

Chapter 2.

1. Buddy meets Billy the Porter.

After deciding he was going to fly to England, Buddy made his way to the airport to see how he was going to make this happen, being a dog 'n' all. He found he could move around the airport without drawing too much attention to himself. It was now that Jon Jon's reading and writing lessons came in useful as he was reading the flight board, he heard a voice.

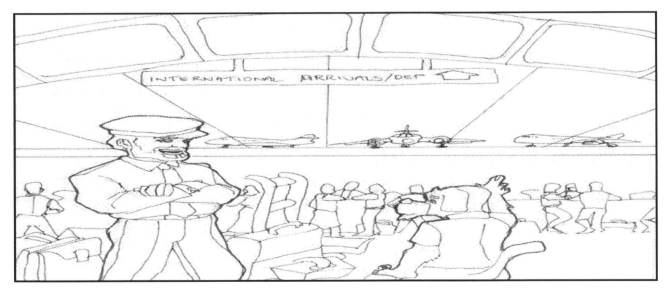

"Hey you! What you doing here looking up at the board like you can read, mind you not looking for something to steal"

"Who me sir," Buddy replied.

"Yes you, who you think I'm talking to," replied the Porter.

"I was checking if Jon Jon's flight come in yet."

Buddy tried to explain, as if the porter would know who Jon Jon was.

"I knew that was you, is you and the lady I had to run out of the airport a few weeks ago."

"O.K! O.K! I'm going you don't have to run me," said Buddy as he began making his way out of the airport.

"I'm not going to run you as a matter of fact I'm glad I see you, I wanted to ask you something."

"What did you want to ask me?"

"That lady who you were with, who is she to you, you live with her?"

"Yes I live with her, what do you want with her?" Buddy asked the Porter with a frown. The Porter could see that the dog was very protective of the lady however, that wasn't going to put him off.

"Don't worry yourself, I don't mean no disrespect, I think she is a very fine lady, I would love to see her again. Can you take me to see her?"

"I don't know; let me think about it… I have to go now I see you soon" Buddy said as he made his way out of the airport.

"Well! Well! What is this? He thought to himself what a turn of events, so the porter (whose name turned out to be William, everyone called him 'Billy the Porter') likes Aunty and wants me to 'fix him up on a date." He could see the benefits of helping this man but he couldn't just fix up Aunty with anybody, he would have to find out what kind of man he was. As he opened the gate to enter the yard he heard Aunty voice calling out to him. "Is that you Buddy?" she asked. "Yes Aunty it's me."

Buddy found Aunty in a good mood, she came out to the backyard with Buddy's dinner and a big bone which she placed beside his kennel and took a seat on the veranda.

"How are you, my little yard dog?" Aunty, asked as she picked him up and put him in her lap so she could pet him while they spoke.

"Aunty when I go to England, will you be lonely?"

"You start with the England talk again?"

"I don't want to go and leave you by yourself. You know Jon Jon wouldn't want me to do that."

"I wouldn't mind some company but at my time of life it has to be the right kind of company."Buddy was surprised at Auntie's response, he thought that she would have dismissed the whole idea as rubbish but she didn't.

2. Up, up and away!

Buddy went back to the airport to look for 'Billy the porter' and told him how he felt about introducing him to Auntie.

"I would have to know that you are a good man and would treat her right". Buddy told him.

Billy must have really liked Auntie as he agreed with every word Buddy had to say. Buddy's love and loyalty for Auntie impressed Billy and they became friends. Buddy took advantage of the friendship by hanging around the airport with Billy so he could find out all he could, about travelling and what it would take to get on one of those planes without anyone finding out. As it happened, one of Billy's duties was to load the luggage onto the plane and he would always let Buddy help him. Billy was a good man, a hard worker who was respected by everyone, even the passengers who used the airport regularly knew him as an all-round good guy.

Billy's tips alone saw him well off, oh yes! Billy was doing alright.

It was time for Buddy to make his move. He mentioned Billy to Aunty, who she remembered, he let her know that Billy liked her and how he thought Billy would be a good friend for her.

Buddy fixed up a meeting, 'it's not a 'date' she would insist 'it's only a 'meeting'. They met and hit it off. It wasn't long before Billy would be coming to the house to pick up Aunty for their dates. Buddy was just glad that she was having a good time.

The only thing he wanted to know was.

"Aunty how come you never let Billy come in the house, when he comes to pick you up?"

"I'm not about to lose my head with some new love and forget what is right, that noisy woman across the road always a watch she never leave from behind her curtains".

"But you like him?" Buddy asked.

"Yes I like him but something's take time, if you going to England you must remember what I'm telling you."

Had Auntie come to terms with Buddy's plan or if by going along with him, she thought he would get it out of his system.

Aunty had underrated Buddy's determination, only Jon Jon knew that was something you shouldn't do.

He packed some food and clothes in his little suitcase, left a note for Auntie telling her to 'take care of herself and not to blame or run Billy away as he is a good man who will take care of her'.

Buddy hid himself in the luggage bay at the bottom of the plane.

When the plane took off the roar of the engines frightened him.

He was in mid-air and there was no turning back, he remembered a saying that Jon Jon's Father use to say 'mind what you wish for, as you might get it'. Buddy was on his way.

3. Buddy meets Little John.

The plane landed at what Buddy thought was London airport. Wrong!
He had landed at the 'John Lennon airport, serving Liverpool and the
North West'. Where is Liverpool? Am I even in England?
Buddy thought, as he looked around.
He decided he had better make his way out of the airport, he didn't want
the dog trapper's to get him, no one knew Jon Jon here.

As he walked and took in the sights, he came to an industrial estate;
suddenly he heard a familiar sound, the wailing of a dog in pain.

It was a similar kind of sound that took him to 'Dog Lane' and looked how that turned out however, he just couldn't ignore the mutt.

He followed the sound to what turned out to be some kind of 'junk yard'. He called out in the direction of the sound.

"Where are you?" Asked Buddy.

"Hurry! I'm over here, this way," replied the voice in the dark. Buddy's senses told him this could be a dangerous place to be, but he wasn't one to leave a dog in distress. He crawled under a car and when he came out at the other side he saw a sight to break his heart. There was a big dog he had been tied up and beaten badly.

When the big dog saw Buddy, his face lit up.

"Come and untie me, be quick they will soon come back." said the big dog. "Who soon come back?" Buddy asked, looking around.

"My boss, that's who, I don't want him to find you here," said the big dog. Just as Buddy was about to move towards the big dog they heard footsteps coming in their direction.

"Quick! Hide." said the big dog.

Buddy could see by the expression of fear on the big dog's face that he should listen, so he slid back under the car and kept quiet.

The big dog's Master went about his business, unaware that Buddy, was watching him. His Master had returned with a bottle in a brown paper bag, which he was sipping from, in between cussing out the big dog and beating him with a baseball bat. "When I tell you to bite someone, you do it you no good mutt," his Master said, which was followed by another blow.

So this is the land of dog lover's? Buddy thought, he felt himself getting angry at what he was witnessing. Before he could stop himself he made a leap right onto the junk Master's back and took a bite out of his neck. The Junk Master cried out, dropped the baseball bat and ran for his life. Buddy untied the big dog and helped him out of the junk yard.

"We had better get out of here, before he comes back with his friends," said the big dog, leaning on Buddy for support.

Buddy was a lot smaller than the big dog and could hardly hold him up. It had been a long day, he needed some rest.

He knew that the big dog wouldn't be able to go on for much longer.

"Don't worry I know a place where we can chill out for a bit," said the big dog.

The big dog took him to a place called Cardboard City. Buddy had never seen so many homeless people living in make shift homes before.

It didn't seem to matter that they were dogs, no one gave them a second look as they put together their own little hut out of the cardboard and old newspaper that was lying around.

Inside their make shift home, Buddy made sure that the big dog was comfortable. He took some of his food out of his little suitcase and gave it to the big dog, he ate it up, with speed and gratitude.

"Take your time, mind you don't choke" warned Buddy.

The big dog didn't even have the strength to answer; he just slowed down a bit, finished the food, thanked Buddy and passed out.

"You sleep my big friend, we'll talk tomorrow."

Buddy assured the big dog as he watched him fall off into a deep sleep. Buddy couldn't help but feel sorry for the big dog, how did he come to be living like this?

Yard Dog could see now how he might seem a bit naive coming to England because it was supposed to be a land of dog lover's; so far he hadn't seen any proof of that. It was only when his thoughts went to Bully dog and his longing to see Jon Jon, did he find his resolve returning. Buddy got some sleep after he wrapped himself in the cardboard and paper. 'Oh, this place is cold' he said to himself as he drifted off to sleep.

4. Where am I?

It was the big dog groaning in his sleep that woke Buddy bright and early the next morning. Buddy had never seen anyone having a nightmare before, he gently woke the big dog.

"How you feel this morning?" he asked the big dog, who groaned something about feeling, a lot better.

"Mi never get your name last night, what them call you?" Buddy asked.

"Did you just ask me my name la?" replied the big dog.

"Yeah, what happen, Yu can't understand me?"

"Just about, where do you come from?"

"I can barely understand you too… I come from Jamaica".

"Jamaica!" repeated the big dog. "You're a long way from home aren't you…by the way my name is John, Little John" said the big dog.

"Off course it is" smiled Buddy, "Yeh, I'm a long way from home." Said Buddy taking a look around him with a weary smile.

"I'm glad you turned up when you did la", said Little John.

"I owe you big time, you saved my life, and you'll find I'm a dog who knows how to re-pay his debts".

"You don't owe me anything, but you can tell me, where am I, where is this place called Liverpool? How far am I from London, and how do I get there?" asked Buddy.

"You are far from London la".

"How far?"

"London is down south, it might as well be ten hundred miles as far as a dog is concerned, how you going to get there?"

"I don't know but you know what they say 'where there's a will there a way'." "Who says that?" asked Little John.

Buddy opened his little suitcase and took out a map, spreading it on the floor. "Show me on this map where London is." Buddy asked, not thinking for a moment that Little John wouldn't be able to read.

"Show you on the map? Do I look like I can read maps, are you joking?" Little John asked.

"Oh, hmm," was Buddy said, not wanting to make anything of the fact that his new friend couldn't read.

"I can read some words; don't get me wrong, I am not thick or anything like that".

"Relax; you think I would be dealing with you if I thought you stupid?" Buddy assured Little John.

"Just checking, so where're going to London then?" asked Little John.

"You want to come to London with me?" replied Buddy.

"I can't let you go on your own, only God knows what kind of trouble you'll get yourself into, what kind of friend would that make me huh?" Little John said with a smile.

"Glad to have you on board" said Buddy, giving Little John a friendly slap on the back, he had forgot that Little John was still a bit sore from the beating he took from his so called Master.

"Ow! That hurt... If we are going to be on the road together, I should know your name".

"My name is YARD DOG!"

"YARD DOG! How'd you get a name like that la?"

"It's not a long story, I'll tell you it one day. Let's hit the road"
said YARD DOG!.

"Yeah lets, we're going to need a ride, follow me". Said Little John.
And off the new friends went into the night, I must say they looked like an unlikely pair but you know what they say about 'judging a book*'.

5. Bully Dog comes to England.

Our little story takes us on board flight, 2169 from Kingston Jamaica, landing at London airport within the next ten minutes. Two of the passengers made quite an imposing sight with their sunglasses and dark suits, looking like 'Men in Black'.

Meet, Detectives Sergeant Brent Woodhouse and his trusted sidekick Constable Kip Johnson.

"Johnson!" called out Sergeant Woodhouse.

"Yes sah!" replied Johnson.

"Yes sir! How many times must I tell you, it's yes sir",

Sergeant Woodhouse corrected his Constable, he was always correcting Constable Kip Johnson's grammar.

"I, I mean yes sir, sah, I mean yes sir".

"Go and check on the dog". Sergeant Woodhouse, ordered Constable Johnson, dismissively.

"But I did just checked the dog sah, I, I mean sir, him alright sir, we will be landing soon sah". Constable Johnson explained pitifully.

"I will go and check, I hope you looked after my dog well, you hear me boy?"

"I looked after the dog good, Mister Bully is alright sir".

"He'd had better be alright, I soon come".

"I soon come,' mimicked Constable Kip Johnson, out of ear shot,

"How I wish him and that dog, who he makes me call 'Mister', would drop through a hole in the plane; the two of them make my life a misery".

Sergeant Woodhouse flashed his warrant card and made his way to the loading bay where they kept the animals, so he could check up on his beloved police dog.

"How are you doing my friend? The fool said we soon land. . . If you are a good boy, I will let you bite him as soon as we get to the hotel, alright Mister Bully?"

Upon hearing his Master was going to let him take another bite out Kip Johnson, Mister Bully, cheered up.

"Oh! You always know the right things to say sir" said Bully Dog, with a big wicked smile.

BUT WAIT! Did we just hear the name 'Bully Dog'? It can't be! Can it? You know what, it really is him, the one and only!

How, did Bully Dog, happen to be on a plane, on its way to England?

Well! We all knew Bully Dog was a Police dog from back in the day; it seems that his old Master who loved him as much as Jon Jon loved and looked after Yard Dog, came back for him after he had helped the dog trapper's get Don Sonny locked up in the dog pound.

Now they were on their way to London, as part of an exchange programme between the Police forces from Jamaica and Scotland Yard. I don't know all the details and if I did, I couldn't say…hush hush you know! It must have been important as Bully Dog didn't even have to stay in quarantine at the airport; Bully Dog just marched right through customs with his Master and Constable Johnson.

When asked, why the Jamaican Police force would send only two Police Officers, they were told they are sending 'the best men for the job' and that seemed to be that. They checked in with Scotland Yard and later that night settled into their hotel, to spend their first night in London, England in 4-star splendour.

Meanwhile, Little John took his new friend, who he knew as 'Yard Dog', to a Lorry terminal where drivers could stop, refresh themselves and break up their long journey.

Most of the driver's weren't at their most alerted state of mind by the time they pulled in to the Lorry terminal get a cup of coffee or tea, so it wasn't hard for the two dogs to jump up onto the right lorry going in the right direction.

"How do you know this lorry is going to London," the newly named Yard Dog asked. Little John took Yard Dog to a sign that said,

'All Lorry's on this side of the docking bay were heading for 'London'.

"What does that say?" asked Little John.

As his new friend began to read it out aloud, Little John joined in unison, showing him that he could read too.

"I just can't read any maps", he Little John said proudly

"Okay, you've made your point, let's get back on the lorry before it takes off without us".

With that Yard Dog got back into the lorry, Little John was still showing off his reading skills, and almost got left behind. He had to run down the lorry with Yard Dog pulling him up just in time, before the lorry picked up too much speed.

"What would I do without you", asked Little John.

"Let's hope, we never have to find out," replied Yard Dog, laughing.

The lorry took off down the motor way with the two dogs on their way to London.

The journey took a lot longer than they both had anticipated and they fell asleep, only to be awakened by a rather irritated Lorry driver.

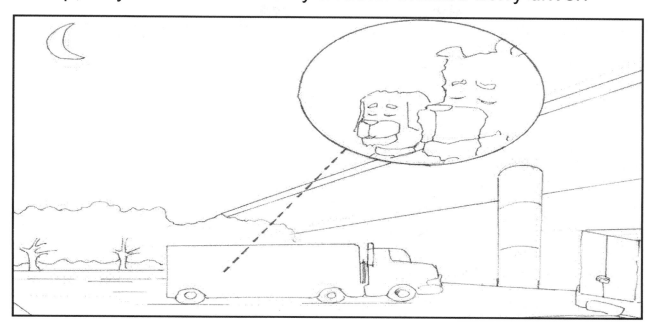

"Oi you two! Out!" he shouted.

When Little John saw the expression on the Lorry driver's face, he wasn't going to take any chances. He started to growl and skin back his teeth as if he was about to pounce.

Yard Dog saw how frightened the lorry driver became, he held back Little John, stood in front of him and snarled at the lorry driver.

It was clear that Little John was traumatized by the abuse he suffered at the hand of his former Master and he wasn't going to let another human or dog for that matter, lay a finger on him. It was a good thing Yard Dog was there to take charge. "Back off boy and let us pass", he told the driver, who did what was asked of him and Yard Dog and Little John jumped off the back of the lorry without any more fuss and went on their way. At the first sign they came to, they found out that they were only a few miles out of London and decided to walk for a bit.

'Come, it's a new day big dog, what don't kill us can only make us stronger, you're safe now', Buddy assured Little John as they 'eased on' down the road, on their way to London.

6. Meet 'One Eye Enos'

Meet 'One Eye Enos' the most confident and mischievous little dog you're ever likely to encounter. Enos sat playing cards with some shady looking big dogs who didn't look the friendly type, you could cut the tension in the air with a knife, Enos hadn't even won a hand but he still manages to pee everyone off. Of course it was part of his plan, the madder he got them, the worst they played; but it didn't seem to be working for him, as they were still winning.

"Your luck is in tonight isn't it?" he ask one of the players who was on a winning streak.

"You've either got it, or you haven't" the dog replied.

"Is that so, huh?" said Enos.

"Well it looks like it, doesn't it?"

"I see what you mean" said Enos, as the dogs was about to pull in another winning hand.

"Wait! Let me see your hand" said Enos. He grabbed the dog by the arm and two cards fell from the cuffs the dog was wearing. Caught! Bang to rights.

"Well, well well! What have we got here? I knew it was too good to be true, you little fart. I knew you were cheating, I just couldn't work out how" said Enos, thinking the house master was going to back him up.

"Grab him, let's show this dog what we do with mutts who see too much" said the other gambler.

They were all in on it, house master too! With that Enos tried to make a dash for it but no such luck. They got Enos by the scruff of his neck and dragged him to the back of the building. I suspect this is where they beat up people like Enos.

"Can't we talk about this fellas, you don't want to do anything reckless now do you?" said Enos.

"You're not talking you way out of this, so you might as well shut up".

"Should we do him?" one of the dogs asked, "let's just beat him up and let him go, I mean we were thieving from him" the dog tried reasoning.

"What! So he can go back and tell everyone how he caught us thieving from him; that would finish us. We would have to move on and I like this ground. I can't tell you when I have ever come across so much fools".

"Is this how I'm going out? Look fella's I'm sure we can come to some arrangement" said Enos.

"You don't hear be quiet!" said the other gambler as he slapped Enos hard across the face.

"Mind the eye, mind the one good eye, what's the matter with you?" asked Enos, who didn't seem worried at all. You have to wonder if Enos knew what kind of danger he was really in.

All of a sudden Little John and Yard dog happened to be passing by, when they came across the 'rip-off posse' who didn't see them; they took in the scene a bit, before deciding what to do.

Enos must have moved something in them as they decided, so many dogs ganging up on one dog because he caught them stealing from him wasn't right and decided to give Enos a helping hand.

"Oi! What you lot doing?" asked Little John.

"What's it got to do with you?" replied one of the dogs.

"It doesn't have anything to do with us, but does it take so many of you to beat one little one eye dog. That's not right," said Yard Dog.

"Who you calling 'a little one eye dog! You just mind your lip, when I done sorting these mugs out you'll be next" said Enos.

Yard Dog, smiled, looked at Little John and said

"I'll say one thing for him, he got heart."

"Yeah I suppose so but just like most cockney's he don't know when to shut up." said Little John.

"You take care of crowd control, I'll get the mutt, cool." said Yard Dog.

"You're the boss! Cool lets go, I've been dying for some excitement."

With that, Little John charged into the three dogs with his big body,

sending one flying with one punch and bit the other one; when the last

mutt standing saw what happened to his two friends he just rolled

himself up in a ball and waited for his licks, crying out.

"It wasn't me it wasn't me, I told them to let him go".

Just as Little John was about to hit him he heard a voice.

"Put him down", It wasn't Yard Dog, it was Enos.

"What did you say?" asked Little John.

"I said put him down now, big boy", repeated Enos.

"Why you little… we just save your neck and you giving me lip?"

"He's not lying, he did try to speak up for me. I'll tell you one more time,

put him down".

With that, Little John dropped the mutt and went after Enos, it was a good thing Yard Dog was there to step in between them; it is safe to say that Enos likes to push things to the edge but for some reason unknown to Little John, Yard Dog saw something in Enos he liked.

"Will you two give it a rest, put him down John" said Yard Dog.

"But we just saved this dog's life and he's talking like he's warning me, like he thinks he wants to do me something" said Little John.

As Little John stood down, Enos started with his 'bad boy' or should I say 'bad dog style' again.

"What! What! What!" he kept on saying with his arms open wide, stepping to Little John but making sure Yard Dog was always near enough to get between them. It was funny to see, as Little John was twice the size of Enos. Yard Dog could see what Enos was doing.

Enos reminded Yard Dog of one of the dogs from Dog Lane.

"Listen, if I was you I would be quiet, you're starting to get on my nerves now" said Yard Dog.

With that last warning from Yard Dog, Enos did as asked and stop talking and started to brush himself down, then he said, "he did try and speak up for me like, he said". He walked up to the mutt, picked him up and went through his pockets to see what he had.

Enos was lucky; it looked like this mutt was the banker as he found enough money to cover his night's losses. Then he pushed him to one side, the mutt got up and ran for his life.

"I am honoured to make your acquaintance," said Enos, holding out his hand or should I say paw to Yard Dog.

'Don't bother with all the fancy talk, what's your name and how you end up like this?' said Little John, who was beginning to hope this little talkative dog wasn't just a waste of time.

"I caught them cheating me at cards".

"You caught them! It didn't look like it," said Little John?

"Well!" said Yard Dog waiting for the rest of the explanation.

"It looks like some people don't like to be caught out, when that one (waving the money he took from him) begged them not to do me; they said they had to, as I might tell everyone about them and they would have to move on," explained the little one eyed dog.

"Talking about moving on, don't you think we should get out of here? He's alright now," said Little John.

"You might be right, let's roll" agreed Yard Dog.

"Well my friend! We'll be seeing you" said Yard dog, bidding Enos farewell. "Where are you two going?" asked Enos.

"No where you can come" replied Little John.

"You don't like me do you?" asked Enos with a smile.

"How did you know," replied Little John mockingly.

"We are going to London," said Yard Dog.

"London! London! Did you say?" asked Enos.

"Yeah, we said London", they said in unison.

"That's my manor, I rule in London, born and bred, under the Bow Bells", he said proudly.

"What is he chatting about, Bow bells?" Yard Dog asked Little John, but before Little John could reply Enos said "Your accent is funny, sometimes I can hardly understand what you're saying. Where are you from?" "Not that it's got anything to do with you but he is from Jamaica, anyway you take care of yourself." replied Little John stepping away from Enos.

7. Two plus One makes Three.

As the two friends made their way down the road, they could feel that Enos was following them. They didn't let on, thinking he would get fed up and go on about his ways. In trying to shake off Enos, Yard Dog and Little John took a wrong turning; they found themselves in a private park. There were some dogs there but they were some posh dogs, when they saw Yard Dog and Little John, they became frighten and ran off. When the posh people saw their posh dogs run away from
 Little John and Yard Dog, they also became concerned and called the 'Dog nappers', who were not like the dog catcher's in Jamaica, Yard Dog found that they always got their dog.

It wasn't long before Yard Dog and Little John were rounded up and flung into the back of the dog catcher's van. As they were about to drive away with the two of them, the dog catcher got another call telling them that there was a sighting of another dog, so they parked up and went to look for him.

"How did we get in this mess?" asked Little John.

"I don't know, if we had someone who knew the grounds, we wouldn't have wondered of the beaten track, would we?" Yard dog, asked Little John, rhetorically. They heard someone playing with the lock of the van door and within seconds the door flew open.

"You two muppets had better get a move on before they come back." said Enos. Just as the grateful dogs were about to jump out of the van they spotted the dog catcher returning to his van.

"Look the trapper is coming back, run." shouted Yard Dog.

This time, the three of them ran off together.

That's how the two man posse became a three man posse.

Enos was as good as his word and showed them how to get to London. Indeed he was some kind of big shot in the London dog sub culture, everyone knew him. In time he and Little John became good friends and stopped going at one another, which made Yard Dog's life a lot easier as he didn't have to keep Little John from doing harm to little One Eye Enos.

When asked how he got a name like Enos, all he could say was his first Master was a 'Reggae fan'. Enos was named after a character from a 'Toots and the Maytals' record called, that's right, 'One Eye Enos'. Oh, by the way, never call Enos, 'One Eye Enos' to his face, he doesn't like it at all, as a matter of fact, he sees it as fighting talk.

As little as he was, Enos would fight anyone, as he would say 'you don't have to always win, you just have to fight'. Yard Dog, always found Enos' cheek amusing but he also always kept an eye on him, if there was ever a dog who never knew when to back down, it was Enos.

At the end of the day, he felt lucky to have found two friends like Little John and Enos. They felt the same way too and they looked up to Yard Dog as their leader; and would follow him to the end of the world.

8. Bully Dog meets Yard Dog.

"Lord! The dog bite me" cried Kip Johnson, "Look how you have you're dog biting me up sir" he complained to his boss.

"Stop going on like a little girl, he's playing with you."

Sergeant Woodhouse loved nothing more than to see his beloved dog bite the one Kip Johnson. He could find no better start to the day.

It was a nice day for walking your dog in the park.

This morning however, Bully Dog had already managed to attack a little dog that some model was out walking. The model had to beat Bully dog off with a stick for the poor little dog's life. Then he went onto scaring the pigeons witless; and as we heard earlier, Bully Dog had bitten his own Master's so called partner Kip Johnson.

Oh yes! Sergeant Woodhouse and Bully Dog were having a wonderful day and it was still A.M.

On the way back to the hotel Sergeant Woodhouse, saw something that he liked in a shop and decided to go and investigate, so he left Bully Dog outside to wait for him.

Meanwhile we find our three friends out walking through central London, "How did you get the van door open?" Little John asked Enos.

"I got skills mate, one day if you're a good mutt I'll show you," replied Enos. Trying to wind up Little John wasn't as much fun anymore as John, learned to take Enos in his stride.

"Well it was a good job you did or this might have been the shortest stay in England for this dog, said Yard Dog

"Where are we now? This place looks alright." asked Yard Dog.

"We are in Victoria, Central London" said Enos. The three friends made their way through Victoria without a care in the world.

Bully Dog, who was still waiting for Sergeant Woodhouse, was looking at the people as they passed him by. This place was a lot different from Jamaica he thought to himself, one thing, 'the people smile a lot more, but they walk so fast'.

All of a sudden he saw a sight…but it couldn't be! 'What would he be doing here, I must be getting home sick.' said Bully Dog to himself.

He rubbed his eyes to make sure he wasn't seeing things.

"Wait! Isn't that Buddy?"

He decided to follow him as it didn't look like the one Sergeant Woodhouse was coming out of the shop for now. Being a former Police Dog, you would have thought that he would know how to tail someone without them knowing, he might have been a bit rusty but let's give him the benefit of doubt.

"I don't believe it, what is he doing in London?" the look on Yard Dog's face spoke volumes.

"You look like you've just seen a ghost la, what is it?" asked Little John, picking up on Yard Dog's concern.

"Don't look behind; just keep walking I'll tell you in a minute".

His two friends did as he asked, they stopped at a park.

"Let's chill out here for a bit, look there is even a drinking fountain" Yard Dog suggested.

They went for a nice cool drink, when that was done they took a seat under a shady tree.

"Come on then la, out with it, how come that dog had you shook" asked Little John. Yard Dog told them the story, the whole story. He went back to a time when he was known as Buddy when Jon Jon was his beloved master, about when he found the place called Dog Lane; he told them everything. The story we all know so well, it all seemed so long ago now, but it wasn't it was just a few months. When the story was over, there was a short silence.

"It seems to me, you and this dog have unfinished business boss" said Enos.

"This is not an everyday thing but I must say I agree with you pal, this dog needs a lesson" said Little John agreeing with Enos.

"What we need is a plan; first we have to find out a few things." said Yard Dog.

"What few things? Let's just do him." said Little John

"We need to find out where he is staying, why is he here? If he's with who I think he is with, we're going to have to be very careful, these are not easy people, trust me." said Yard Dog.

"Okay, let's put a plan together." agreed Enos, looking at Little John and shaking his head.

They did put a plan together, as plans go it wasn't a great plan, but it did the job. This time they followed Bully Dog, only he didn't know he was being followed. They found out that he was in London with Sergeant Brent Woodhouse, who Yard Dog knew.

The good Doctor Ford was Sergeant Woodhouse's Doctor back home and as such, Sergeant Woodhouse would sometimes come to the house on Palm Lane. Yard Dog also knew how hard this man could be, the Jamaican Rude boys were very frightened of this man.

That aside, the three man posse found it easy to lead Bully Dog into a trap. Enos got a girl friend of his, to lead Bully Dog to an alley way in the heart of Soho, at the back of the Yip-Yap club, where Yard dog and his crew made their base and also took their name the 'Yip-Yap crew' which was given to them by the local shop keeper's, who loved to see 'Yard Dog' and the 'Crew' dancing to the music coming from the club at night. The queuing customer's would always throw money and the local butcher always made sure they were well fed. Anyway back to the story.

Now they had Bully dog back at their base Little John tied him up and they waited until Yard Dog arrived.

The way Enos was laying it on thick, Bully Dog was expecting to see the 'Dog Father' turn up.

"Who this Yard Dog you keep talking about?" asked Bully Dog.

"What do you mean you don't know who Yard Dog is?" asked Enos, who seemed to be enjoying himself. Well, he always saw himself as a gangster, he could keep this line of interrogation up all night.

"I said I don't know anyone by the name of 'Yard Dog', I came here to meet a girl." Bully Dog tried to explain.

Just as he said that, in walked 'Pretty Cleo'.

"Do you mean me, big boy" she said, laughing.

"Oh! You set me up! What do you lot want with me?" asked Bully Dog.

"Of course it was a setup, you think you could pull a girl like that" asked Enos, pointing at Pretty Cleo.

"You just sit there and wait, if you're a good boy we might let you go, Come Cleo, let's go and get something to eat". "No, let's wait for Yard Dog, we can all go together", replied Pretty Cleo "That's true", agreed Enos.

Now I'm tied up in god knows where, waiting on god knows who, someone named Yard Dog, Bully Dog thought, all he knew, If he didn't get back to the Hotel he was staying in with his beloved master, Sergeant Woodhouse, he might think he has run off; and go back to Jamaica without him. He would be stranded in England what would he do then?' Bully Dog wondered as he struggled with the ropes that tied him to the chair.

In walked Yard Dog, when Bully Dog saw him, he asked

"Wait! It's you, they call Yard Dog?"

"Yes it is me they call Yard Dog, I have you now'.

What should we do with him boys?" asked Yard Dog.

"Let me have him, let me have him", begged Enos.

"I say, we just wait until tonight and drop him into the Thames who's going to miss him?" said Little John. Bully Dog began to get frightened knowing he was at the mercy of Buddy, who for some reason everyone now called Yard Dog and who seemed to be 'carrying the swing' around here.

"I have to go and see Jon Jon, let him stay here until I come back," said Yard Dog "Which Jon Jon is that, Jon Jon Ford? You had better be able to swim or fly, Jon Jon and his family have gone back home to Jamaica." said Bully Dog, laughing.

"You are a liar", said Yard Dog, grabbing Bully Dog.

"I should leave you here and let Enos take care of you."

"Go and check if you think I'm telling you lies, he's gone back to Jamaica" said Bully Dog. "Listen, let me go and I will never trouble you again, I beg you".

"You just wait till I come back, you had better hope they haven't gone back to Jamaica." said Yard Dog before he set off with Little John.

They went to check out the address Yard Dog had for the Fords; and low and behold Bully Dog wasn't telling lies. They had found out that Jon Jon and family, was staying at the address but have gone back to Jamaica, something to do with the death of Mrs. Ford's older sister.

"Oh no! Aunty dead!" Yard Dog said, as he made his way back to base, with Little John where they had left Bully Dog tied up.

"Come on Boss, we can cry about your Aunty later. We had better get back to base, who knows what Enos will do to Bully Dog if we leave him alone with him for too long." reasoned Little John.

"True" said Yard Dog, they picked up their pace. It wasn't long before they got back to base, where they left Enos, Bully Dog and Pretty Cleo. Oh excuse me! Do forgive me; allow me to introduce the one and only 'Pretty Cleo'.

She lived up to her name, a real 'Poodle Mama' anywhere you went with Pretty Cleo you can be sure she would always attract a crowd, everyone loved her it was something to see, people would pet her and make a fuss; when Yard Dog first saw it, he realized, it was true, England really is a land of dog lovers. Pretty Cleo however only loved one person and that was Enos. Enos loved Pretty Cleo too but not in the same way; he loved her and looked out for her, like a big brother.

It didn't matter how badly he would treat her, or how they would fight, she would never leave him; as tough as she was and Pretty Cleo was tough! She would only take crap from Enos.

So now, you have met the one and only 'Pretty Cleo'.

Yard Dog and Little John walked in as Enos was slapping Bully Dog. "What are you beating him for, you think you could beat him so if I untied him," asked Yard Dog.

"You should have heard what he called Cleo, no one talks to her like that mate, no one," replied Enos, angrily.

"Yes okay, but no more violence, you seem to like the rough stuff too much, just chill out," said Yard Dog.

I don't know what it was but Enos never argued with Yard Dog, never.

"You where right, they have gone back to Jamaica, Aunty is dead." Yard Dog said to Bully Dog shaking his head with sorrow.

"What are you going to do with me?" asked Bully Dog.

"The way I feel right now, you are lucky that I don't let Enos done you; but in honour of Aunty, I'm going to let you go but let me tell you this, if I ever see you again . . ."

Just before he could finish, Little John said "Boss you can't let this dog go, if you do you will always have to look over your shoulder."

"I hear you John but I want you to trust me on this one." insisted Yard Dog. "Alright! You must know what you're doing," said Little John, "Enos, untie him." Little One Eye Enos untied Bully Dog and the four of them took him out of town and left him in the middle of nowhere, with a warning not to come back to London, Bully Dog promised, he never would but you know who a promise is a comfort to? That's right, a fool!

Off Bully Dog went, to try and find his way back to the hotel, he was also just glad to be alive as he knew if it was him he wouldn't have shown so much mercy.

Yard Dog was still reeling from the news that Aunty had passed on.
But he was going to be alright, he had his boys and one girl who were there for him. Fate had brought him to London, England, and he decided this was his new home now, and these people were his new family.
He would always love Jon Jon and the Ford family and it took some time before, thinking about them didn't cause him a little pain and longing.

Little John would remind him he was a dog and he belonged with them.

Enos would tell him to stop being a 'cry baby' and 'man up'.

You know only Enos could talk to Yard Dog like that.

As for Bully Dog by the time he got back to the hotel, he had found that Sergeant Woodhouse had thought he had run off; and as his time in England had come to an end, he and Constable Kip Johnson, had to go back to Jamaica right away. They were needed, the 'Rude Boys' back home, were being very, very Rude!

Bully Dog ended up in Battersea Dog's Home where after a time he ran away and swore vengeance on Yard Dog and his Yip-Yap crew.

'If they had never kidnapped me' Bully Dog, reasoned, he would have got back to the hotel in time and his beloved Master would have never gone home without him. 'I bet you the one Kip Johnson, told him to go and leave me… wait till I see him, I am going to bite him too; but first I'm going to mash up the one Yard Dog and his Yip Yap crew, if it takes me the rest of my days', vowed Bully Dog. That was one very angry dog!

Meanwhile, back at the alley-way, where Yard Dog and the Yip-Yap crew hung out.

"Hey guys! You hear that Bully Dog is back on road, la?" asked Little John.

"A true?" Asked Yard dog, as he put down the news paper he was reading.

"Its true," replied Pretty Cleo.

"You just make sure you're careful, you know he's going to want to see you" said Enos, to Pretty Cleo, showing concern for her well being.

"He can come and see me, whenever he wants… I can take care of him" she said, with a confidant smile, batting those big eyelashes.

"I'm sure you can, but like Enos said, be careful… that dog can be very mean and we don't want to lose you, now do we, what would the Yip-Yap crew, be without you," said Yard Dog, as he smiled and kissed Pretty Cleo on her forehead.

With that everyone laughed and another day started for Yard Dog and the Yip-Yap crew. All of a sudden the music from the Yip-Yap club, started to rock the Alley-way, and Yard Dog the Yip-Yap Crew, began to sing and dance.

'We'll soon see you, you'll see us too, so Yip-per-de Yap with the Yip-Yap Crew! As they all danced down the road and off into the sun set.

And that is where our story ends for now. So we'll say later to Yard Dog, Little John, Enos and the one and only Pretty Cleo!

But if you're lucky you can follow Yard Dog and the crew every week. Trust me!   Yip-Yap! For now.   THE END!

The Philosophy, Words and
Wisdom of Yard Dog.

....

Throughout this story of adventure and discovery, our hero 'Yard Dog' is guided in moments of doubt and despair by the words of his former master Jon Jon Ford. These words of wisdom and Philosophy were passed down to Jon Jon Ford by his father, the good Doctor Ford.

Now I don't claim that these sayings are made up or written by the good Doctor and his son, I don't say they are written or made up by me; but as the story is peppered with them throughout, I thought it might be nice for the reader if we collect them all and put them in a list for you.

Like I said 'you never know when you might need words of wisdom to guide you in trying times. So be good, live long, enjoy your childhood while you can (as you will be adult for much longer than you are a child) prosper, peace and out'.

1) You have to know how, to get on with all kinds of people, from all different walks of life.

2) Duppy knows who fi frighten.

3) If you feed a hungry dog, it will always come back.

4) Familiarity, breeds contempt.

5) Let your word, be your bond.

6) Whenever you dig a pit for your brother man, don't dig one

   always dig two.

7) Think, before you act.

8) Mind what you wish for, as you might get it.

9) A promise is a comfort to a fool.

10) Yu fi tek time, tek yu head, out of the lion's mouth.

11) Where there's a will, there's a way.

12) Don't judge a book, by its cover.

Glossary of Jamaican Terms and Idioms.

Mek	Make.
Yuh	You. (singular)
Unu	All of you.
Fi	For.
Lawd Gad	Lord God.
Mi	Me or My.
Duh	Do
Em	Him.
Nuh	No.
Teef	Steal or Rob.
Pickny	Small Child.
Wah	What.